A NORTH-SOUTH PAPERBACK

Critical praise for

The Other Side of the Bridge

"The story follows an engaging little boy named Andy on his quest to find springtime. It's the middle of a snowy winter, and Andy longs to see signs of the coming season. Andy is a nature lover and can spend hours studying flowers or even the tiniest of spiders. The other boys in the neighborhood tease him about being different, but little Andy, a fearless guy, teaches us a thing or two about bravery and what is really important about friendship acceptance."
American Bookseller "Pick of the Lists"

"This is a suitable selection for young readers venturing beyond the easy-reader stage."
School Library Journal

Wolfram Hänel

The Other Side of the Bridge

Illustrated by Alex de Wolf

Translated by J. Alison James

North-South Books

NEW YORK / LONDON

First published in the United States, Great Britain, Canada,
Australia, and New Zealand in 1996 by North-South Books,
an imprint of Nord-Süd Verlag AG, Gossau Zürich, Switzerland.
Distributed in the United States by North-South Books Inc., New York.
First paperback edition published in 1999.

Library of Congress Cataloging-in-Publication Data is available.
A CIP catalogue record for this book is available from The British Library.
ISBN 1-55858-626-1 (TRADE BINDING)
3 5 7 9 TB 10 8 6 4 2
ISBN 1-55858-627-X (LIBRARY BINDING)
1 3 5 7 9 LB 10 8 6 4 2
ISBN 0-7358-1203-9 (PAPERBACK)
1 3 5 7 9 PB 10 8 6 4 2
Printed in Belgium

For more information about our books, and the authors and artists
who create them, visit our web site: http://www.northsouth.com

Andy was not the kind of boy who ran
out to play sports every afternoon. Instead
he liked to study nature, and would stand
at the window for hours watching the
leaves fall or a spider spinning a web. He
knew the names of all the trees, and all
the birds that built their nests in them. He
even knew how to identify animals from
their tracks.

The other boys teased him, especially
Big Jon. He was twice as big as Andy, and
more than twice as strong.

"Hey, squirt!" Big Jon would say. "You
forgot your growing pills again!"

But Andy just walked away.

One day Andy told his father, "I'm
going to the woods."

"What are you going to do there?"

"Look for spring," explained Andy.

"Well," muttered his father, not quite knowing what to say. "Don't go too far, and come back in time for dinner."

"I always do," Andy said, and he pulled his hat down over his ears.

It was cold. And it was drizzling. But that didn't bother Andy. Yesterday he'd found the first sign of spring, a snowdrop pushing its way out of the cold ground. It wouldn't be long before other flowers were blooming too.

Andy took the path down to the river.
The water gurgled and splashed over the
smooth rocks.

Andy walked along the narrow river
path under the tall pines. He walked for a
long time, until he reached an old wooden
bridge. It was so old, it had lost one
handrail, and the other looked like it
was about to go.

Andy sat down on the big rocks by the bridge. He pulled off his boots and tested the water with his toes. Brrr! It was icy!

A squirrel hopped from branch to branch overhead, chattering loudly.

"Don't worry," said Andy. "I won't hurt you."

Andy put his boots back on. He
wondered what it was like on the other
side of the river. He had never been
over this bridge. Nobody had. Not even
Big Jon.

And Big Jon was so strong he could break a piece of wood with a chop of his hand. He wasn't afraid of anything . . . except crossing this bridge, because on the other side lived Old Jasper. There were terrible stories about Old Jasper. Big Jon said he ate children for breakfast. Andy's aunt insisted his cat was a witch. Nobody ever saw him. He lived alone in the woods.

"So what?" thought Andy. "I won't go far. I just want to see if spring has come on the other side of the river."

Andy went over the bridge.

There! A couple of white windflowers. And right next to them were three cowslips, bright as yellow sunshine!

Andy went a little deeper into the woods, finding flowers all the way. He didn't notice the sky growing dark. He didn't notice the cold. He didn't notice when the rain pricked like fine needles.

Suddenly Andy looked up. What was that?

Snowflakes! Andy couldn't believe his eyes. "It's snowing in the springtime!" he said.

The snow fell thicker and thicker. The snowflakes danced and swirled, and Andy spun around watching them until he got quite dizzy.

"I'm cold and I'm hungry," he said. "It's time to go home."

But which way was home? The path had disappeared, and so had the flowers. There was nothing but white snow everywhere.

Andy started through the trees. But everything looked different. This wasn't the right way. He turned to the left and kept walking, but that was wrong too. He turned again. Then he saw his own footprints. He was going in a circle.

He was lost.

Now Andy was afraid. His feet were
numb with cold, and the cold was
creeping up his legs. His fingers were so
cold, they were stiff. He felt in his pocket
for his carrot. That would help.

Just as Andy went to take a bite, a rabbit hopped up to him through the snow.

The rabbit stopped right in front of the boy and looked frightened.

"Hello there," Andy said sadly. "Are you lost too?"

Andy broke his carrot in half. One
piece for him, one for the rabbit.
   The rabbit munched.
   Andy munched.
   For a moment he felt better.

Gently Andy picked up the rabbit and held him under his arm. The snow kept falling, covering Andy and the rabbit like white fur.

The snow fell in Andy's face. It stuck to

his eyelashes so he couldn't see. It stuck to his nose so it was hard to breathe.

"This is terrible," said Andy.

Blindly he fumbled through the woods from tree to tree. Branches snapped and scratched his face. His hands were scraped and poked with thorns. He tripped on a big root and fell facedown in the snow.

The rabbit rubbed its nose on Andy's.

"Sorry," said Andy. "You'll have to find your own way. I'm too tired."

The rabbit laid back its ears and hopped away.

The snow kept falling, thicker and faster.

Soon Andy was nothing more than a little hump in the endless white.

Andy lay still, as if he were dead.

But he wasn't dead. He was having a wonderful dream. He dreamed that he was as tiny as the flowers, and the flowers had faces, like people. They were so kind, they picked him up and brought him to their court. They undressed him, and put him in flower robes, and laid him gently in lamb's wool. The sun was warm, the flowers were singing like birds, and . . . Andy woke up. The birds were singing, and the sunlight was on his face. There was no snow. He was warm and cozy in a big bed, in a little log cabin. He took a deep breath. It smelled like . . . spring!

Just then the door opened. In came a
man. A big man, with a wild beard and
a shirt full of holes.

"Time for breakfast," said the man, and he cracked some eggs and threw some bacon into the giant frying pan on the stove.

Suddenly Andy knew where he was. This was Old Jasper's house. He was supposed to eat children for breakfast— not bacon and eggs! Andy wondered if he should run away.

But the delicious smell of frying bacon pulled him out of the soft bed, and Andy realized he was as hungry as a bear.

They sat down at the table, and Andy ate without stopping.

"Hope I cooked the eggs right," Old Jasper said. "Don't get much company around here."

"They're wonderful," Andy mumbled with his mouth full.

Jasper wasn't so terrible after all. He had friendly eyes. And his cat, who rubbed against Andy's legs and purred, was just a cat, not a witch.

"You were darn lucky," said Jasper. "You have to be careful this time of year. A sudden storm like that is dangerous. And the worst thing to do is lie down and go to sleep. You might never wake up."

"But you found me," said Andy, smiling.

"Fritz brought me to you," explained Jasper. "Fritz is my rabbit."

Then Jasper was quiet.

Andy scraped the last bits from his plate.

Then they went outside.

Fritz came hopping up and wiggled his
ears. A couple of goats peered curiously
around the corner of the house, and
somewhere hens were cackling.

"Ahem." Jasper cleared his throat, and looked up at the sky. "If you want to come back, we could do a little fishing down at the river."

Andy pointed out a tiny purple flower. "Look!" he said.

"Violet," said Jasper. "First this year."

Andy smiled at his new friend.

Jasper brought Andy back to the bridge. He waved good-bye, and disappeared into the woods.

"Thank you!" called Andy. "I'll come back soon."

Jasper's voice drifted through the trees. "Bring some worms for fishing . . ."

"I won't forget," whispered Andy.

Suddenly, coming down the path on the other side of the bridge was Andy's father! "Andy!" he shouted.

Andy ran over the bridge and into his father's arms.

"We've been searching all night," his father said, as a group of men gathered around. Even Big Jon was there.

"Thank heavens you're safe. We were beginning to think . . ." but he couldn't say any more. He was so happy, he was crying.

Andy laughed and said, "I found spring, and I met a friend with a beard this big!"

On the way back Andy told them what
had happened. He stopped to point out
each new sign of spring. "See that crocus?
Look, a robin finding worms. I have to
bring worms when Jasper and I go fishing."

Big Jon pulled Andy aside. "Hey," he said. "How do you know so much about birds and plants and things?"

"I can teach you," offered Andy.

"Hmm," Big Jon said.

"Did you really spend the night at Old Jasper's place?"

Andy nodded happily.

"And he'll take you fishing?"

Andy nodded again.

Big Jon asked, "Could I come too?"

"Of course," said Andy. "We just have to bring the worms."

About the Author
Wolfram Hänel was born in Fulda,
Germany. He trained to teach English and
German, but he decided not to go into
teaching. Instead, he began to write plays
and stories for children. His previous
books for North-South are *Jasmine and
Rex*, *The Extraordinary Adventures of an
Ordinary Hat*, *Lila's Little Dinosaur*, *Mia the
Beach Cat*, and *The Old Man and the Bear*.
He has two homes: one in Hannover,
Germany, and one in Kilnarovanagh,
Ireland.

About the Illustrator
Alex de Wolf was born in a suburb of
Amsterdam. He studied at art school, and
because he liked drawing children and
animals, he often sat for hours sketching
at the zoo. Alex de Wolf lives with his
wife and two young sons in Amsterdam.
For North-South he has illustrated *Lila's
Little Dinosaur* and *Melinda and Nock and
the Magic Spell*.

Other North-South Paperback Easy-to-Read Books

Abby
by Wolfram Hänel
illustrated by Alan Marks

Bear at the Beach
by Clay Carmichael

The Birthday Bear
by Antonie Schneider
illustrated by Uli Waas

**The Extraordinary Adventures
of an Ordinary Hat**
by Wolfram Hänel
illustrated by Christa Unzner-Fischer

Jasmine & Rex
by Wolfram Hänel
illustrated by Christa Unzner

Leave it to the Molesons!
by Burny Bos
illustrated by Hans de Beer

Lila's Little Dinosaur
by Wolfram Hänel
illustrated by Alex de Wolf

**Little Polar Bear and
the Brave Little Hare**
by Hans de Beer

Loretta and the Little Fairy
by Gerda Marie Scheidl
illustrated by Christa Unzner

Meet the Molesons
by Burny Bos
illustrated by Hans de Beer

Melinda and Nock and the Magic Spell
by Ingrid Uebe
illustrated by Alex de Wolf

Mia the Beach Cat
by Wolfram Hänel
illustrated by Kirsten Höcker

Midnight Rider
by Krista Ruepp
illustrated by Ulrike Heyne

More from the Molesons
by Burny Bos
illustrated by Hans de Beer

A Mouse in the House!
by Gerda Wagener
illustrated by Uli Waas

The Old Man and the Bear
by Wolfram Hänel
illustrated by Jean-Pierre Corderoc'h

On the Road with Poppa Whopper
by Marianne Busser & Ron Schröder
illustrated by Hans de Beer

Return of Rinaldo, the Sly Fox
by Ursel Scheffler
illustrated by Iskender Gider

Rinaldo on the Run
by Ursel Scheffler
illustrated by Iskender Gider

Rinaldo, the Sly Fox
by Ursel Scheffler
illustrated by Iskender Gider

Spiny
by Jürgen Lassig
illustrated by Uli Waas

The Spy in the Attic
by Ursel Scheffler
illustrated by Christa Unzner